Tikiri

Copyright

This is a work of fiction. Names, characters, businesses, places, events and incidents are either the products of the author's imagination or used in a fictitious manner. Any resemblance to actual persons, living or dead, or actual events, situations, and customs is purely coincidental.

The use of any part of this publication, reproduced, transmitted in any form or by any means electronic, mechanical, photocopying, recording, or otherwise or stored in a retrieval system without prior written consent of the publisher—or in the case of photocopying or other reprographic copying, a license from the Canadian Copyright Licensing Agency—is an infringement of the copyright law.

• • • •

THE GIRL WHO CROSSED the Line
    The Red Heeled Rebels Series
    Prequel
    All rights reserved.
    Copyright ©2020 Tikiri Herath
    Edition: 2020
    www.RedHeeledRebels.com[1]

• • • •

LIBRARY & ARCHIVES Canada Cataloging in Publication
    ISBN: 978 0 9939616 5 6

• • • •

AUTHOR: TIKIRI HERATH
    Publisher: Nefertiti Press
    Copy Editor: Stephanie Parent

---

1.   http://www.RedHeeledRebels.com

Cover Design: Angela Oltmann
Back Cover Headshot: Aura McKay

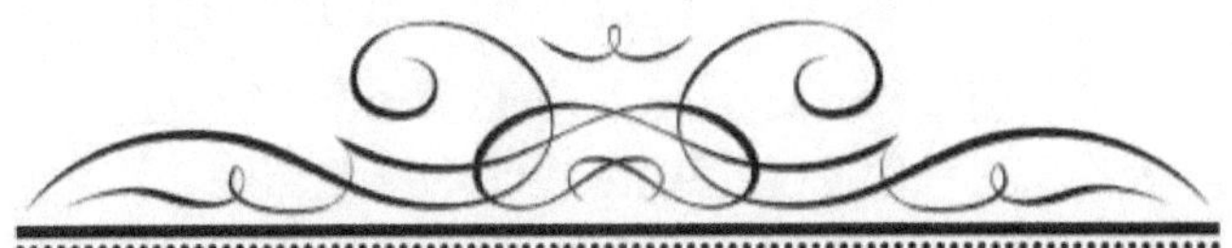

The Girl Who Crossed the Line

Prequel to the
Red Heeled Rebels Series

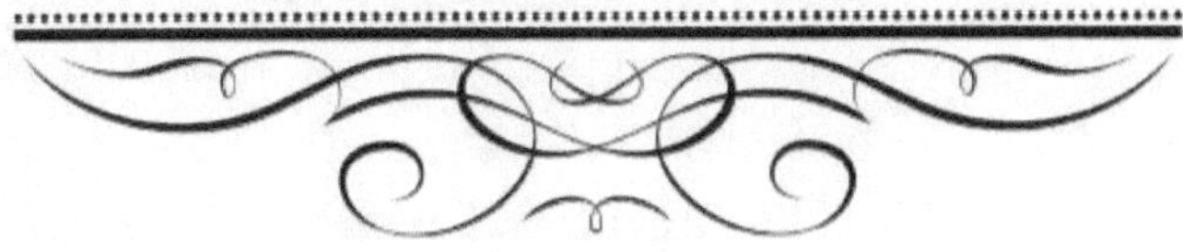

Formerly titled SHATTERED / BEGINNINGS

Other Titles by Author

<u>The Red Heeled Rebels Thriller Novels</u>[2]

The Girl Who Crossed the Line
The Girl Who Ran Away
The Girl Who Made Them Pay
The Girl Who Fought to Kill
The Girl Who Broke Free
The Girl Who Knew Their Names
The Girl Who Never Forgot

• • • •

The Accidental Traveler

An Anthology of travel short stories based on the author's sojourns around the world.

• • • •

<u>The Rebel Diva Nonfiction Series</u>[3]

Your Rebel Dreams: 60 Days to discover your purpose and passions and power up your life.
Your Rebel Plans: 30 Days to create a masterplan for your career and life change.
Your Rebel Life: 100 habit hacks to transform the ten most important pillars of your life.
Bust Your Fears: 3 easy tools to conquer your fears and upgrade your career and life.

• • • •

Collaborations

The Boss Chick's Bodacious Destiny Nonfiction Bundle

---

2. http://www.RedHeeledRebels.com

3. http://www.rebeldivas.com/

Dark Shadows 2: Voodoo and Black Magic of New Orleans

The door banged open.

I looked up, startled.

Who's coming in now?

I peeked through the crack in between the two bookshelves.

A gaggle of girls in private school uniforms had stomped in and were taking over the table at the center of the library. They hadn't noticed me behind the shelves, watching.

I held my breath. I knew if they ever found me here, I was finished.

Pens and journals came flying out of expensive designer bags. Someone unrolled a large white sheet of paper in the middle of the table. All heads bowed over it. Like they were planning to invade China.

The librarian had stepped out for lunch that day, asking me to keep an eye on things. As she always did. She knew me from the countless hours I spent at the library of the international school in Tanzania. She always had a recommendation for her "little Indian bookworm," as she called me.

There was an old rocking chair in the back of the main room, near the window. The librarian and I had a quiet understanding. This was my chair, my corner, at least during lunch hour.

Hidden behind the bookshelves, I spent every lunch hour in this chair, curled up with a book, munching on my onion buns, monitoring things. With the sun streaming through the window and warming my shoulders, it was a cozy place to be.

As I watched the girls around the table now, I burned with curiosity.

"Do we have a place yet?" Tanya asked, breaking the silence.

Tanya was the tallest girl in class. With a pretty face and ebony skin, she was the one everyone said would become the next Naomi Campbell.

What impressed everyone most was Tanya's father was none other than the American ambassador to Tanzania. And that meant, her word ruled all. From hearing my parents debate world news every night at supper, I couldn't help feeling my class was a miniature United Nations, including the power-play that happened between the countries.

"My home is open to you," replied Zuwena with a bright smile.

The girls squealed with delight.

"My father says we have to finish by midnight but he will allow it. He even agreed to open the pool for us."

"Oh, my god, you're the best," said Tanya, squeezing Zuwena's arm. "That's super awesome."

Zuwena's parents were influential politicians in the country. Her mother was often on television, giving fiery speeches, and her father was often in the newspapers shaking hands with foreign dignitaries. They were always traveling for work with an entourage in tow which meant Zuwena's home was the best place to host a party.

I'd never been to her home myself, but everyone talked about her "house" at school. Zuwena lived in an enormous estate surrounded by a tall brick wall. Inside the sprawling compound, her parents lived in the main residence while she and her siblings each had their own smaller detached houses with dedicated servants and cleaners to look after them.

Judging from the excited looks on the girls' faces, there had to be some truth to this rumor.

"Do we have a caterer?" asked Tanya, moving down on the agenda, all business.

"I got that covered," Bethany replied. "Mother's favorite caterer will bring us treats. They catered to the queen's birthday celebration last month and everybody was delighted."

Bethany's father was a high-ranking official in the British diplomatic corps in the country, and their embassy parties were the most lavish in town. Or so I'd heard.

"That's super, Beth," said Tanya.

"Don't you all want to know what we'll be having?" Bethany asked, glancing around at her friends.

"Yes!" a chorus of voices replied.

"Tell us!"

Bethany cleared her throat. "To start, we'll have cucumber sandwiches, mini quiches, crab cakes, prawns on sticks, caviar jackets and plates of cold meats and rare cheeses."

Satisfied murmurs went around the table.

"And for dessert, we'll have lemon bars, butter scones, blueberry shortcake, swiss rolls, and a fancy chocolate cake smothered with Belgian chocolate icing."

"Oh, my goodness."

"Sounds divine."

"Delicious."

From my corner of the room, I looked down at the last bite of the onion bun in my hand. It had lost any appeal it had had.

I half wished I could join the girls, but I knew how they'd react if I'd asked to enlist in their exclusive club. A pang of jealousy went through me.

We couldn't be more different.

Uniformed chauffeurs drove these girls to and from school in shiny black Mercedes. And I took the bus. At lunchtime, they bought burgers, chips, and ice cream at the canteen using their unlimited pocket money, while I ate homemade onion buns from a brown paper bag. These girls flew to London, New York, and Johannesburg for their vacations, while I spent my holidays in my family's two-door, forest-green Fiat in the back roads of the African savannas.

How I envied them.

Our differences were not just in lifestyles, but also in what our parents did for a living.

Every morning in class, I'd sit next to the kids of politicians, diplomats and wealthy business people who ran the biggest mining syndicates in Africa. They owned the cattle ranches, the airlines, the railways, even the shipping lines. While their parents worked hard to keep their businesses on the continent, mine investigated those same businesses' environmental and labor practices.

At the dinner table, I often heard my parents talk about the companies that belonged to their families. I couldn't help but wonder if my classmates' parents talked about mine around their dinner tables too. I suspected they did because no one wanted to hang out with me at school.

The only places where I felt welcome were at the library and in my martial arts class.

When I was learning to kick, punch, and jab at Bob the rubber man in the gym's corner, I was equal to everyone else. Our instructor didn't judge us by the clothes we wore or how many cars our families owned. All we had to do was show up in a T-shirt and shorts and follow the rules. It was my favorite class and my kicks came fast and furious even though my legs were shorter than anyone else's.

When I wasn't at the gym practicing kicks or in class, learning, I hung out at the library. I could stay there for hours with my best friends whom I found between the pages of books. Books were my escape whenever I felt sad or lonely. They took me on adventures and let my imagination soar. As long as I had books for friends, I didn't mind too much being the black sheep in school.

But it was that day, as the girls whispered conspiratorially over the library table, that I learned what they really thought of me.

"What else do we have?" Tanya asked, looking around her party committee.

"Aunt Majorie just got back from Jo'burg and brought me these beautiful packets of French macarons." Sophie, the French girl in my class, piped up. "I have hundreds of them in all colors. It will be my pleasure to share them with you."

Sophie had her golden hair in pigtails and her signature pink lipstick on. When she introduced herself to the class on the first day of school, she made sure to tell us all about her father's mining company in East

Africa. This inspired our teacher to introduce a new word to us: m-o-n-o-p-o-l-y.

I'd recognized the company because my parents had inspected it for Environ Africa.

One night, my parents were cleaning up in the kitchen, talking in low voices. We'd just finished supper, and I was doing my homework at the dinner table. But I couldn't help overhearing them.

Whenever my parents' voices dropped, I knew the topic at hand was "adult conversation," one I wasn't supposed to hear.

So, that night, I put my pencil down, leaned toward the kitchen door and listened in.

"**T**he supervisors beat them. They're not even eight and they send them down those mine shafts," my mother was saying. "It's a terrible thing happening right under our noses. Just children, I tell you, *children*."

"No one cares as long as they're making money," my father said. "We did what we could do."

"You think telling the commissioner will solve this? Sometimes I wonder if he's with them. Politics over people is what always happens."

"We did our best," my father replied in a grave voice. "Even James quit and went back to Texas. He was getting those threats too, you know. Maybe we need to start looking too."

What threats? I wondered.

"Well, we don't have any other place to go," my mother said with a sniff. "This is our home now and we need to do what we can right here."

"Remember Sven from Norway? They said he died hiking in the desert. I know him. I *knew* him. He hated the outdoors. He lived in the lab, even on Sundays. Someone didn't want him talking."

"Oh, yes, I remember. So pale, like he'd not seen the sun in his life." My mother sighed. "But we don't want to get carried away now. Maybe, he went out for a walk and got heatstroke or something."

"Dirty business over science, more like it," my father mumbled.

They were silent for a minute.

I was just about to turn back to my homework when my mother spoke up, her voice slightly higher pitched than before.

"This is a serious accusation. So serious I don't even want to think of it."

"Those men from the Boko Mines came to see me yesterday," my father said slowly as if choosing his words with care. "Four men in that black armored jeep they always drive around in. They were smiling and friendly but one of them had a gun. I saw it on his belt. I think he wanted me to see it."

Boko Mines? Didn't that belong to Sophie's family?

I slipped out of my chair and tiptoed toward the kitchen. I peeked in.

My father was facing the sink.

"Some days," he was saying, as he settled a washed plate in the dish rack, "I wonder if they...."

"Not now," my mother cut him off, giving me a sideways look. She'd spotted me slinking near the doorway.

With a guilty look on my face, I stammered, "Hey, can I have some cake? Please?"

"Go finish your homework, child," my mother scolded, shooing me out with her dishcloth.

"Karma will get them eventually," my father said, not even looking up. "They can't go on like this forever."

It was a conversation that would haunt me later.

But that night, I had nightmares of Sophie in her golden pigtails dragging me to an underground mine, to work in a deep, dark place where no one would find me. I avoided her like the plague from then on.

• • • •

"SOPHIE, YOU'RE A GEM!" Bethany said. "I love macarons. How lovely of you."

"They come in so many gorgeous colors," Sophie said. "I can't wait to show them to you."

"You can't get anything like that in this dump," said another girl. She gave Sophie a friendly nudge. "You're a star, you know that?"

"*Mon plaisir,*" Sophie said with a smug smile.

"What about drinks?" Tanya asked. She always kept everyone on track. "We've got to have drinks. Serious drinks, ladies."

"I've made plans for punch," Ana said, sitting up, proud to be doing her bit. Ana was from Spain and came to school with her five brothers in a limousine. "My brother said he'll ask our driver to get wine for us. He's got connections at the duty-free shop. No one will find out."

"Hey," Shanti said, with a worried look on her face. "Please don't get caught. If my father ever finds about the drinks at the party, he'll never let me talk to you again. Ever."

Shanti was the doe-eyed daughter of the Indian High Commissioner and the only other Indian girl in school.

She was prim and proper, except for the oversized earrings that dangled dangerously from her earlobes. She bought her clothes from Harrods in London, where she went shopping every three months and dined on sweet gulab jamun balls sprinkled in gold dust. Real gold. I knew this because she reminded me every time we met.

I wished she'd be nicer with me. I had the same waist-length black hair and chocolate-brown skin she had. I'd never had a sister and had always wanted one, but she took pains to remind me how different I was from her whenever she could.

"Okay, what about the invitations?" Tanya asked.

"Got everyone," Bethany said.

"Hope you didn't invite *that* one," Sophie said.

"Gosh no, I'd never do that," Bethany said.

"Who are you talking about?" Ana asked.

"The little tramp," Sophie said wrinkling her nose.

"You mean the stick insect?" Ana said.

I almost dropped my book.

I'd always been skinnier and smaller than my classmates. The boys in class taunted me with "runt" or "stick insect." The latter particularly troubled me because I was frightened of insects of any kind, and images of my arms turning into long-legged jabby things haunted my dreams many a night.

"You mean the other Indian girl?" Tanya asked.

"She's not Indian!" Shanti spoke with such vehemence, it surprised me. "She's only half-Indian, and that's lower than the lowest caste. Trust me, I know these things. I'm from the Brahman caste."

"Whatever you say," Tanya said with a shrug. "You know these things."

"Shanti's right," Sophie said. "She's a mulatto. Her mother's from some island or something."

"Hey, do you know the mulatto's mother sells cakes at the market?" Bethany said.

I felt my face go warm.

"No!" a chorus of horrified voices replied.

"Our cook saw them at Uhuru last Saturday," Bethany said.

"Who buys cakes at the market?" Sophie said with a sniff.

"Who *sells* cakes at the market?" Ana said.

I stopped breathing.

"She doesn't belong here," Tanya said, her voice almost sympathetic.

"Don't her parents work for that environment company or something?" Ana asked. "Mother says they're worse than hippies."

"Why do they let riffraff in here?" Bethany said. "Why can't she go to the local school, whatever it's called, down the road?"

"No idea, but I know why she smells so strange," Sophie replied. "She's always playing with the locals and eating smelly stuff."

"Dresses weird too," Tanya said, "like she's from a hippie commune or—"

"A slum," Shanti said.

Chapter THREE

T he rancid smell from the slums was suffocating.

It always was, when we drove through the south side of the city. The smell of open sewage pipes and mountains of garbage came to us well before we saw them. I usually put my finger on my nose and held my breath till my mother yelled, "Close the window, child, before I have a stroke or something!"

I'd roll up my window as fast as I could, slam back on my seat, and let out my breath in one giant whoosh.

I liked to leave the car window down, even when it rained. This way, I could stick my head out, feel the wind in my face and take everything in.

When we were in the city, I'd watch out for buses loaded with people, packages, baskets, spare tires, and even mattresses. When we drove to remote mining towns, I'd keep an eye out for lone trees in the middle of a vast, barren land, or rustic villages with mud huts scattered along desolate roads.

I'd see village women dig their fields with handmade hoes, chanting soulfully, lulling the babies strapped to their backs to sleep. Other times, I'd see girls half my size stumble along the road, balancing aluminum pots of water twice their size on their heads. I always waved at them. They always waved back.

Then, there were days when I'd sniff the warm, dusty air in anticipation of catching a hint of the smoky, fishy aroma of the Uhuru Market.

Ever since we'd moved to Tanzania, our Saturday afternoon forays to the market had become my weekend treat. This was the largest open-air marketplace in the outskirts of Dar es Salaam. My parents and I spent hours chatting with people, nosing around the stalls and buying our weekly supplies straight from the farmers.

I looked forward to Saturdays, not because it was a getaway from the routine, but because the Uhuru market was where my best friend lived.

As soon as my father found a shady spot to park our Fiat, I'd jump out and race toward the open stalls. My only goal was to find Chanda wherever she was hanging out in the market that day.

Though my mother was from Sri Lanka and my father was born in Goa, India, to everyone in the market I was the "little Indian girl." Being different meant every market boy and girl was curious, but only a few ventured to say hello.

Girls peeked from behind their mothers' skirts, pointed and smiled. Boys laughed at my hair, some daring to pull my ponytail before running away, giggling hysterically. Chanda, the local hairdresser's daughter, was exactly my age and was the first one to invite me to play. Soon, the market became our Saturday afternoon playground, where we ran wild and free.

When I hung out with Chanda, I felt like I belonged. I felt like I'd finally found a friend in this world.

We'd spend most of the day skipping through the stalls. We'd hold our noses as we passed racks of dried fish on old newspapers, smelling like the Maldive fish jars in my mother's kitchen, except a hundred times worse.

We'd navigate through mazes of brown barrels, so large I had to get on my tiptoes to see inside. They were mostly filled with rice grains or coffee beans, but sometimes we'd come across strange things like the green bottle gourd that was like a cucumber made for giants, or the yellow-horned melon, whose gooey, snotty insides made me gag every time someone cut one open.

Chanda and I would dart in and out among tables laden with spice baskets, practicing the martial arts kicks I'd learned in school that week, and which I'd happily taught my friend every weekend.

But if we peeked inside the baskets, we'd see chocolate-brown cinnamon barks, dark fingers of cloves, ginger roots, vanilla beans, spiky lemongrass, and a myriad of other roots, herbs, and barks that promised everything from adding flavor to curing the most incurable maladies.

Right in the middle of the market, we'd encounter the charcoal bar-becue racks, their delicious smoky smells rising in the air, making my stomach rumble. Here, teens armed with steel tongs would holler at us to buy a skewer of marinated mutton or a grilled chicken leg. They knew my parents, and their wallets were not far away.

There was only one part of the market we weren't allowed to go.

Chanda's mother called it the "forbidden place," and forbade us from venturing anywhere near it. But that just made us more curious. We'd skirt around the section, wondering what made it so special.

This was at the edge of the market where glassy-eyed chickens lay with their feet tied together. It was also where young goats kicked, bleat-ed, and pulled on the harnesses that tethered them to tree stumps.

I couldn't bear to look them in the eye, knowing they'd be flipped on the barbecues soon. But those poor animals never crossed my mind when I pleaded for a skewer of meat at lunchtime, much to the chagrin of my vegetarian mother.

My mother was particular about everything.

She always wore the same outfit, a white blouse, navy pants, and flat black pumps, whether she stayed at home, was at work in her office or went to the market. But in the back of her wardrobe were two Sri Lankan saris, one made of dark pink lace and the other of peacock blue chiffon, both of which she kept folded and sprinkled with mothballs. "They're for special occasion days only," she used to say with a firm voice whenever I begged to see them, touch them.

In contrast to my mother, the women in the market made every day a special occasion day.

They wore their full-length, printed kangas, making the markets a bright canvas of eye-popping colors. Canary yellows and navy blues mixed with emerald greens and flowing reds. Inexplicably, lime green lines interwoven with yellow polka dots looked beautiful. On their heads, the women donned wraps with oversized bows, their colors and styles jumping out, shouting out.

Like these clothes, nothing was muted in the market. The women bustled around with their wares, cleaned their displays, called for their kids, and bartered their goods loud enough for the world to hear.

It was these beautifully dressed women who manned the markets of Africa.

They'd sit on roughly hewn wooden stools behind their stalls, fanning themselves with the Saturday newspaper and gossiping with their neighbors. The men, I found, normally sat at a makeshift pub under a corrugated aluminum shelter arguing about politics, holding on to warm bottles of beer. I never saw them do anything. So, to my child's mind, the women were the bosses of the market. How could they not be?

Buying anything from these bosses of the market involved certain rituals.

When we arrived, the stall owners would clap their hands in greeting and offer us rooibos tea. The buying happened much later, after a chat about the weather, everyone's families, and the latest news of the day. My mother would sip her tea and browse the wares while my father would try to make a deal on whatever we needed.

But the market women were a formidable force, and they always outnumbered him. First, they'd gasp in horror. "Be serious, Bwana!" they'd say and call their girlfriends from nearby stalls to come and see this reckless foreigner who'd named such an irrational price.

My father detested haggling and was sure everyone took advantage of him. So he'd stand with his hands behind his back, looking officious in his tan safari suit, sticking to his price, a price he thought was supremely reasonable. The African women towered over his diminutive frame, debating, laughing while he refused to budge. I used to think he'd stand like that till dawn, if not for my mother's trick.

Once she felt the deadlock had gone long enough, my mother would walk back to the car and pick up her tray of fairy cakes. Then, in front of the curious crowd, she'd open the cover with a flourish.

My mother, a chemist, was unassuming by nature, until the day she discovered Julia Child on TV.

After that, she couldn't resist imitating her idol, especially when she uncovered her baked goodies in front of a group of lively spectators. With oohs and aahs, the women would jostle each other and gather around to see what cakes my mother had made that day. These small cakes with colorful swirls on top became our currency at the market.

Later, when we got home, I'd discover buried at the bottom of our baskets a ripe mango or two, a small bottle of oil, precious cinnamon sticks or a handful of cloves. Gifts from the bosses of the market.

I wished every day could be a market day.

Chapter FOUR

Visiting Chanda at the market was like going to the circus.

I never knew what to expect, but I knew it would be fun.

Chanda's father was a migrant miner whose name she didn't know. She only knew he was from Zambia and had left them and moved back when she was just a baby.

Mrs. Ngozi, her mother, was the market hairstylist. Every morning, she laid out her shiny, polished tools on her bench as early as five, before the hustle of the day began. There, she sat all day, cutting and snipping, straightening and braiding the hair of the market women.

The day I met Chanda, my mother had decided it was time to trim my uncontrollable mane.

"You're starting to look like a jungle girl," she'd said, looking me over with her hands on her hips. So, that afternoon, she left me in the care of Mrs. Ngozi while she went off to sell cakes at the bread booth. Mrs. Ngozi got down to snipping, and in fifteen minutes had tamed my hair.

"There, done!" she said, with one last stroke of her comb.

That's it?

I wanted more. I pointed at the girl playing hopscotch in front of the booth, the girl with broken red sandals and shoulder-length braids in multicolored ribbons. Every time she skipped, those braids flew in the air like a mini-rainbow.

I wanted the same rainbow braids.

Mrs. Ngozi shook her head.

"Impossible, my dear. Your hair doesn't have kinks like hers," she said with her hand over her mouth. I was sure she was laughing at me, but that wasn't going to stop me. I crossed my arms and gave her my most stubborn pout—the one that worked so well on my father.

"Oh my, oh my. You want hair like my Chanda?" She pointed at the girl, who was now watching me with a pixie glint in her eye. Mrs. Ngozi ruffled my hair and shook her head again. "Can't be done."

I didn't budge from my stool.

"Please, Mrs. Ngozi?"

"Are you going to sit and sulk here till I do, little one?" she asked.

I nodded.

"Okay," she said with a sigh. "Okay. If that's what you want, that's what you'll get."

I beamed at her, uncrossed my arms, and sat up straight to let her do her job.

"What will your mama say, huh?" Mrs. Ngozi said, massaging my hair vigorously with shea butter oil. "Did you think about that?"

I sat as still as I could, while my head jerked from side to side as she pulled my hair apart with fast, skilled hands and with such force it brought tears to my eyes. I blinked them away quickly, hoping she wouldn't notice.

"She's gonna think I'm messing with her baby's hair, that's what," Mrs. Ngozi muttered, more to herself than me. "She will *kill* me, and then you, you stubborn girl."

It took a whole hour before the final ribbon-tying began. By then, Chanda had gotten bored with her solo game and was watching her mother work her magic on me. She gave me a cheeky grin and put her tongue out. I didn't dare move, not wanting to interrupt her mother's work.

Once Mrs. Ngozi was done, she swiveled me around on the stool. Round and round I went, my new braids with their colorful ribbons swirling in the air. I couldn't help giggling.

Chanda jumped up and down laughing. "You look so funny!"

"Oh, yes?" Mrs. Ngozi said to Chanda. "She looks exactly like you now."

Someone bent down to touch my hair. "Freshi, freshi!"

Mrs. Ngozi turned to her friends, who were now gathering around to see what the fuss was about. "Will you look at that? I didn't think I could do this with *Wahindi* hair."

"Nice job!" one woman said, clapping her hands.

"Bomba! You're so talented."

"Maybe you should try *Muzungu* hair next!"

Mrs. Ngozi looked away with a bashful smile. "*Asante*," she said with a slight dip of her head.

"*Asante*!" I echoed with a big smile. "Thank you, Mrs. Ngozi!"

"You little devil," she replied, pinching my cheek. "Now go tell your mama you forced me into this. Go!"

I looked over at Chanda. "You wanna come with me?"

Chanda didn't say a word but came right over. Hand in hand, we skipped through the crowds toward the bread booth, our colorful braids flying in the air.

"You tell her it's free, you hear!" Mrs. Ngozi shouted after us.

Chanda knew the market like the back of her hand. She knew where everything was and said hello to everyone we met.

Except for one man.

At the edge of the market, near where the chickens and goats were tethered and where we weren't allowed to go, sat a fat, grumpy man. He sold everything from the latest electronic gadgets to candy and chocolate in eye-popping wrappers and beautiful shoes of every color and shape. His stall was chock-full of curiosities you couldn't find anywhere else—expensive curiosities Chanda and I drooled over.

This man, with a belly like a buddha, wore a long white nightgown, in contrast to the bright and colorful shirts the other men at the market wore. On his head was a black and white scarf held down by a thin black band. His skin was lighter than the others, so everyone said he was a foreigner from somewhere up north.

We always found him in the same position on his mat, legs crossed, counting a string of beads with his left hand, and flipping an ancient book with his other hand, mumbling to himself. For someone who sold nice things like sweets and shoes, he wasn't a very nice man. If he caught sight of a child near his stall, he yelled and cursed till his face turned red.

"He eats kids for dinner," Chanda whispered to me one day and broke into peals of laughter at my horrified expression. I didn't fully disbelieve her.

But we couldn't help ourselves.

This shop had all the wonders to stoke a little girl's curiosity. Every Saturday afternoon we snuck behind a nearby tree stump and gazed at the rows and rows of shoes on display, salivating over them like they were diamonds, telling each other which ones we'd buy if we had the cash.

All I owned was a pair of black school shoes and a pair of brown house slippers. All Chanda had was one pair of broken red sandals tied together with string. We dreamed of the ruby red sandals stacked in the bottom of the shoe rack.

"That's what I want," I said, pointing at them. "Me too!" Chanda said.

Late on Saturday afternoons, when the market was getting ready to close, we'd linger near the old man's stall just a bit longer. We hung around because that was when mysterious things happened here. That was when we'd find a row of beautiful young women standing in front of the stall, waiting for something.

Some came alone, some came with their parents, or so we thought. At first, we were sure they were waiting in line to buy those fancy shoes and jealously wondered what special deal he was giving them. But then, we noticed the girls never looked happy or got to pick their shoes, or even looked at the shoe rack.

They stood like lifeless dolls, while the man pointed at some of them, one by one. Then, the older people would walk up and get papers from him. Sometimes, we saw money being exchanged. Sometimes, the chosen girl would collapse to the ground and cry. It was a strange scenario every week, and we never figured out what it was about.

Chanda was sure the girls were being chosen to become the old man's wife. "All of them?" I asked, to which Chanda had no answer. I thought the girls were being chosen to become famous fashion models in foreign magazines. "Why do they look so sad then?" she asked me, to which I had no answer.

Talking about this with Mrs. Ngozi only made her furious we'd ventured into the forbidden part of the market.

"He's a bad man and those are bad girls," she said, wagging a finger at us, her beautiful face scrunched into a dark frown.

She looks more scared than angry, I thought.

"I don't want you two anywhere near that place, you hear me?" she said, raising her voice—something I'd never seen her do before. "Didn't I already tell you girls this?"

"But why are those girls bad, Mrs. Ngozi?" I asked, overcome by curiosity.

She looked away. A dark shadow flickered across her eyes. "Those girls are exiled from the village."

"Exiled?" I said, trying out this new word.

"What does exile mean, Mama?" Chanda asked. "Did they do something bad?"

"Stop asking silly questions and go play. But you go near that stall again and I will be very angry. And when I say don't go, I mean it!"

And that was that.

Asking my parents the same question brought threats of getting banished to my room forever if I stepped near that area again.

But Chanda and I had little willpower to stay away from the only stall in the market that carried the most beautiful things we'd seen.

Chapter FIVE

E very night when my mother tucked me into bed, I imagined Chanda sleeping between sacks of hay and beans at the market. In my mind's eye, I saw her waking up to cockerel crows in the morning and playing among the stalls, all day long.

What a dream life she has, I thought.

Carefree, easy, without worries of mean girls or difficult homework. It was only when Mrs. Ngozi invited my family for supper a few years later, that I learned how Chanda really lived.

That afternoon, while Chanda and I played, Mrs. Ngozi hauled out a pumpkin, carved it into pieces and threw them into a large blackened pot simmering on the fire pit. While my parents chatted with her, she mixed in more vegetables and chili.

Their home was a one-room hut with mud walls and a corrugated aluminum roof, an hour-and-a-half walk from the market along a pot-holed road. They had no electricity or plumbing and used candles inside the house at night and a common well in the center of the village for water. Their stove was an open fire pit outside their main door.

Our dusty little Fiat parked by the side of their house looked foreign, even extravagant.

After letting the food cook for a few minutes, Mrs. Ngozi brought out a mysterious pouch from inside the house. She measured a tablespoon of the coarse brown powder and let it fall like a waterfall into the bubbling pot. I squeezed in between my mother and her to peek in. The smell of saffron and cinnamon filled my nose. The air smelled earthy, spicy, sweet.

A half-hour later, we sat under the shady banyan tree next to their home, feasting on sweet potato pumpkin stew served with rice on bent aluminum plates.

It was an evening I'd never forget.

On our way home, my mother turned to my father and said, "It's always those with the least who give the most, isn't it?"

Those with the least? Chanda's playground was the entire market. She had everything a girl could dream of, except those ruby red slippers from the old man's stall.

"Mama," I said, looking down at my own boring black shoes. "I really need new shoes."

"What's wrong with the ones you have?"

"They're getting old," I said with an overemphasized sigh.

"But we got those only six months ago."

"I need sandals, Mama."

"Goodness, child, first you go get your hair braided without telling me. Now, you want sandals? What's got into you?"

"They're comfier and I know where we can find nice red ones."

"You don't need more shoes."

"Even for my birthday?"

"But that's not for three months."

"Promise you'll get me red sandals? Please? *Papa?*" I knew appealing to my father meant better odds.

"Well, if you really want—," my father started.

"We'll see," my mother interrupted.

"For a birthday present, why not?" my father said. I knew he'd not want to antagonize my mother, but I also knew he knew how to convince her. He looked at me via the rearview mirror. "If that's your birthday present this year, will you promise to do your homework every night?"

"Yes!"

"And promise not to bother Mama about shoes again?"

"Promise!"

I grinned.

My mother was quiet, but I knew I'd won. *Those pretty shoes will be mine soon.* But I wasn't done yet.

"Can we get a pair for Chanda too?"

Silence.

"Her sandals broke, so she has to tie them with a string now."

My mother made a funny choking-like noise. It was neither a yes nor a no, but it told me she was listening.

"Then Chanda can walk to school easily," I said.

"Hmmm," my father said. My mother cleared her throat but said nothing.

It was then something strange struck me.

I saw Chanda only on Saturdays and had no idea what her weekdays were like. Whenever I brought a book with me, which I always did, she'd ask to borrow it and devour it within hours, only to ask for more.

The strange part was she never had her own books and never complained about her homework like I always did. She seemed to live her whole life in the market. In fact, she had an obsessive interest in hearing about my school, which I hated to talk about, especially on weekends.

"What school does Chanda go to?" I asked out loud.

"She doesn't," my mother said, looking out the window, into the distance.

"I thought everybody's supposed to go to school."

"Asha, my dear." My mother paused and let out a sigh. "We send you to school so you can get a good education. You are a lucky girl."

"But I hate it. I just want to play in the market like Chanda."

"How can you say that?" my father said, throwing a hand up in the air. "You're learning in English. You will get an American high school diploma and even get to do British A-levels. Do you know what that means?"

"Yes, Papa," I said in resignation. I'd heard this lecture before.

"This means you can go to any university, anywhere in the world."

"But the girls are mean to me," I said.

"Why do you let those silly girls worry you so?"

My father was looking at me in the rearview mirror, his forehead lined with concern. "Keep your head down, study hard, and you'll see the fruits of your labor before long. Who knows? When you grow up, you will become a doctor, a lawyer, an architect or even an accountant. Imagine, Asha, how proud that would make us."

Ah, yes. My destiny had been defined since birth.

It was doctor, lawyer, architect, and accountant. In that order. My preference was to become either a martial arts fighter or a baker, but my parents would have none of that. To join a respected profession was, to them, the pinnacle of existence. To go to school was the only job a little girl had.

I was now a pro at going to schools.

By eleven, I'd attended five schools in four countries—Tanzania, Kenya, Zambia, and Nigeria, not counting a three-month stint in Namibia and a single month in Zimbabwe where my parents worked at a uranium mine. This meant I had to adjust to different classes and teachers continuously, and it hadn't been easy.

Most of my teachers were foreign expatriates. They worked in international schools for a year or two before moving onto another country, another continent, or often back to their homelands. I liked most of them, but it was Ms. Stacy from Canada, who taught grade six at the International School of Dar es Salaam, who gave me a lesson that would save my life many years later.

She was the youngest teacher that year. With a happy-go-lucky smile on her face, she was friendly and approachable. In her early twenties, fair, and plump with a blonde bob cut, she couldn't have been more different from me, but we shared a bond. Our love for reading.

She was the one who, whenever she visited the school library, brought down juicy books from the top shelves for me. It was she who introduced me to Oliver Twist and Robin Hood. Looking back, it was she who taught me how to think for myself and to stand up for myself.

I still remembered the day I handed in my first book review to her.

"I didn't want you to summarize the book, Asha. I wanted you to critique it," she said.

I looked at her, worried. She looked at me, worried.

My heart sank. My parents expected me to do well in school. No, they demanded it. They gave me time to adjust to a new school, but from previous experience, I knew three months was pushing it.

"But Papa said Jules Verne's the best writer in the world. There's nothing to critique."

She gave me a thoughtful look. "Whether he's right or wrong, you need to come up with your own idea of it. Think for yourself. Don't follow anyone's opinion blindly."

How could she imagine Papa could be wrong?

I didn't like everything my parents made me do, like when they made me go to bed by nine every night, but I was confident they knew everything there was to know about the world. They were scientists, after all.

"I'll give you two extra days to rethink this, okay?" Ms. Stacy said. "Give me something new. Tell me how *you* would write this book."

I glanced at the book on my desk, an old copy of *Around the World in Eighty Days*, its title hardly visible on the faded cover. When I announced my need for a good storybook for homework over supper, my father rooted through his small library to find the "perfect" one. He carried several books with him wherever we moved — tattered tomes, barely readable, most torn, but his treasures. This one was his favorite, so I had turned the first page with great expectations.

"Once upon a time," the book began. And with those four magical words, the room around me receded, and I slipped into another world.

Once upon a time, the book said, an English man named Phileas Fogg travels the world to win a bet he'd made with friends. Together with his French valet Passepartout, he rescues a young Indian princess called Aouda who'd been on her way to die by fire at her dead husband's pyre. The three of them team up and cross continents to arrive safely back home in time to win the wager.

By the time I'd turned the last page, I had become Princess Aouda. With her raven hair and chocolate-colored skin, she looked just like me,

I imagined. It was the perfect story to get lost in, a story of friendship and courage, of places beyond imagination, one that only the greatest writer in the world could conjure up. It had become my favorite book too, and for the life of me, I couldn't find anything to criticize.

After two sleepless nights and a chewed-up pencil, I wrote a one-page essay to Ms. Stacy.

The adventures of Fogg and his friends had mesmerized me, but one thing was glaringly missing. I was certain Fogg loved his plum puddings, Princess Aouda her gulab jamuns, and Passepartout his cherry crêpes, but imagine the exotic culinary adventures they must have encountered along the way, just as my parents and I did on our travels.

I salivated at the possibilities.

That oversight was pretty careless of the mighty Verne—a missed opportunity to spice up his book. Somebody, I wrote, should put a recipe book together for the countries Fogg and his companions had visited. Better yet, I wrote, somebody should make the best sweet desserts from each country they'd traveled to and sell them at the Uhuru market just like my mother did with her fairy cakes.

Ms. Stacy liked my answer.

"Atta girl. That was what I was looking for. An amazing idea. I see entrepreneurship in your future," she wrote on my paper with a smiley face next to it. I had to look that word up in the dictionary that day.

"Hey," I said looking up at my parents in front, "Why can't Chanda come to my school?"

I imagined the two of us playing in the schoolyard and at the gym, huddling over books in my secret corner of the library, even sharing my onion buns. At last, I'd have a friend to hang out with at school.

Silence in the front seats.

"Do you know why Papa teaches at the university after work?" my mother said finally. "And why I make cakes for the market?"

I gave an obstinate shrug.

"It is so we can make extra money to send you to the best school. Poor Chanda can't go to school because Mrs. Ngozi doesn't have much. If we could afford to pay for her school too, we would do that in a heartbeat."

"Listen," my father said, using his serious voice, "I want you to promise me something."

I waited.

"I want you to promise me you will finish school no matter what. Do you understand?"

That, I knew, wasn't a request. "Yes, Papa."

"Promise?"

I nodded.

But my mother was already changing the topic. "I can't wait to start our vacation. I really need a break from this place, you know."

"Me too," my father replied, nodding. "Those goons from the mining company can't bother us while we're on holiday."

I didn't realize then how fateful those words were.

Chapter SIX

I was halfway through my homework the next night, alone at the dinner table when I learned of my parents' plans.

My stomach was full of spicy grilled eggplant, a crispy green bean stir fry and the yellow fried rice with peas my mother liked to make on Friday nights. These Friday night dinners weren't great for an alert mind. I was barely keeping awake.

My parents were in the kitchen, cleaning up as usual. In between their conversation, I could hear the chink of china and the squeak of the faucet as it opened and closed.

My school books covered the dining table. I liked to spread myself when I did my homework because it made me look and feel busy, even if I wasn't progressing very far. And that night, I was desperately sloughing through an algebra exercise, dozing over my books, wishing I was elsewhere.

"Did you hear from the embassy?" my mother asked.

What embassy?

"They didn't reject us yet," came my father's voice in between a cupboard being opened and shut. "If all goes well, they'll ask us to come in for a security check soon."

Their words wafted toward me through the kitchen door, my mind half on the math puzzle in front of me and half listening in to what was going on in the kitchen.

"Security check?" asked my mother.

"Fingerprints, photographs and all that. We'll also have to sign a paper to agree on them doing criminal checks in every country we lived in."

"How long will that take?" My mother sounded worried.

"A few months if we're lucky. We'll have to be patient. They have a process in place to make sure everyone's checked out before they emigrate."

Emigrate?

I'd heard that word before. That sounded serious. I wondered what my parents were up to now.

"So, you think it's promising then?"

"Hard to say. I'm doing everything I can."

I wondered vaguely where we'd go to next.

Back to Kenya where I was born? To Botswana where I'd heard they have amazing safaris. To Namibia? Zimbabwe? Or maybe to South Africa? I felt a jolt of excitement go through me. I'd heard Johannesburg had shopping malls the size of a city and I'd never been to a real shopping mall before. Then, maybe Shanti would stop thinking I'm a girl from the slums. Maybe I could invite Chanda to visit me or maybe even stay with us so she could get to see the big city too.

My father let out a sigh. "There's so much paperwork to do and we'll have to wait a long time, but I know it's worth it if we get in."

"That's true," said my mother, "At least, Asha will get to go to a high school in America."

I sat up.

America?

"It will be safer there for her too," said my father, "and for us."

America, like the America Tanya comes from?

I was on full alert now. I put my pencil down and turned to look at the open kitchen doorway.

I couldn't see my parents bustling inside the kitchen but I could hear them. I badly wanted to walk over and ask them what they were talking about, but I knew that was the fastest way for them to clam up about the whole thing for good.

"I want to see her in a good university," my father was saying, "maybe in medicine or law."

"Or technology," replied my mother, "there are good jobs in the tech sector these days. Well-paying ones too."

I shook my head and pinched my wrist, just to make sure I hadn't fallen asleep on my math book and was dreaming all this.

Are they seriously thinking of moving to America? Like the United States of America?

My heart ticked faster.

"I'd be happy if she got into accounting in a small college even," said my father, "something stable. Something professional, you know."

Study hard, get all A's, and become a doctor or a lawyer or an accountant. If I'd heard it once, I'd heard it a million times. What was new, what made my heart race and my imagination soar was the thought of doing this in America.

This was a country I'd read about, I'd dreamed about, I'd watched on television riveted, thinking how lucky Tanya was to come from such a glamorous nation where everyone was happy and rich. It was the best place on earth, or at least it seemed to me because whenever anyone wanted to leave a country, they all wished to go to America. Every one of them.

I considered my options.

Disneyland was what came to mind first. Shanti and Sophie had already been four times and bragged about it every time. Then, there was the Grand Canyon, a picture of which hung on my classroom wall. I wondered what kind of animals they had up there. I knew they didn't have lions, cheetahs, zebras or elephants. I made a mental note to look up a book on American geography the very next day in the library.

I debated whether to gulp down my glass of water so I could make an excuse to walk into the kitchen and fill it up. Then, I thought, I could ask an innocent question or two and wiggle out more information from my parents.

"I'd love to see New York," my mother was saying. "Though it may be too expensive for us."

New York!

I almost choked on my glass of water.

"We'll probably have to look for jobs in a smaller town first," said my father. "Maybe somewhere in the mid-West and then work our way to Boston or somewhere where they have good schools."

"I read in the news the other day that Nashville is booming," said my mother. "They're looking for professionals. Not many immigrants in Tennessee but with our science degrees, we should be fine, no?" I could hear the anticipation in her voice mixed with a slight tinge of nervousness.

My very particular mother rarely got excited, so this must mean a lot to her too.

"Once we get the green light, someone from the embassy is supposed to help us find the best places to settle," said my father. "They want immigrants to go to places where they don't have many workers. Stimulate the economy and all that, you know." His voice turned somber. "But don't forget we'll have to take a demotion at the beginning. We have to be prepared for that."

"I know it's not going to be easy. When Kamala went to Canada with her family, she had to redo her bar exam. I think she was a legal secretary for years till she got back into law. It's a sacrifice. That's for sure."

"But it's all for a good cause," replied my father. "It's good for Asha and we won't have to worry about her so much."

I felt a thrill go through me. *I have the best parents in the world.* Another thought struck me. *Maybe, just maybe, if Tanya, Zuwena, Sophie, Shanti, and Ana knew I was going to America, they'd invite me to their parties, invite me to join their exclusive club.*

"The best thing about this is we get away from these criminal thugs," said my mother, her voice sounding cold and angry now. "This really shouldn't be happening, you know. I feel like they're chasing us away. They want us to go away, don't they?"

"We're the lucky ones," said my father in a sober tone. "We'll find a way out."

He lowered his voice.

I leaned in further.

"It's the kids in the mines, I don't know what to do about. Think of it. They've got nowhere to go. No family. No home. No country."

Chapter SEVEN

My parents never broke their promises.

On my birthday morning, I found a pair of red sandals at the foot of my bed. Shoes they'd found at a department store in town.

When I showed my prized possession to Chanda at the next Saturday market, her eyes grew wide.

"Wow! So beautiful," she whispered in awe, running her fingers across the straps. That afternoon, she stopped me every ten minutes to examine my shoes and say, "You're so lucky." Every once in a while, she stooped to look wistfully at her own broken sandals.

I realized then how much she wanted what I had, just like I'd always wished for what Sophie, Tanya, Zuwena, and Bethany had. I hated the idea that Chanda probably felt in my company what I felt in theirs. I couldn't bear the thought of us having this difference, a difference that would separate us, I was sure.

It took me only ten minutes to decide what I had to do.

I pulled Chanda by the hand and ran over to the edge of the market, toward the forbidden place where the old man had his stall. I told my friend in a firm voice to stay at our usual hiding spot behind the tree stump until I give her a signal.

My instructions had been clear. I was on a mission.

While Chanda stayed behind, burning with curiosity, I tiptoed over to the edge of the old man's kiosk.

His head was hung low over his book as usual. The candy jars were laid out in a row on the table to his right. In the middle of the kiosk was a plastic table piled with a jumble of electronic gadgets of every kind. On his left was a treasure trove of shoes. Beautiful shoes. There were yellow ones, blue ones, black ones, with buckles, bows, and polka dots, and even a purple pair with two-inch heels.

But I trained my eyes on the red sandals in the corner, the ones that looked a lot like the new pair I'd received from my parents that morning.

The man muttered to himself as he flipped a page.

I froze.

But he didn't see me or hear me. I turned my head to look back at Chanda and glimpsed a scared brown eye peeking from behind the tree stump. I lifted my hand up to say "stay exactly where you are."

I turned my attention back to the stall. The old man was still bent over his book. I was so close, I could see the stringy lines strung across the pages, looking like fancy art rather than words I recognized.

I waited another ten seconds.

The man soon nodded over his book. He was falling asleep.

It was now or never.

I took a step forward. Then another.

If he opened his eyes now, he'd see me. I didn't have time. I reached out in a flash and clawed the smallest pair of sandals.

A thundering crash made me jump. I'd pulled the entire shoe rack to the ground.

I fled.

"Oi!"

I didn't look back.

"You black rascals!" The man's incensed voice came from behind me. "I will skin you alive!"

"Run!" I yelled.

Chanda darted out of her hiding spot like a bullet.

"Wait till I get my hands on you, you filthy mongrels!"

Chanda and I didn't stop to find out. We ran through the stalls, dodging people, benches, umbrellas, and dogs. We ran without stopping until we got to the other end of the market, until we could run no longer.

Then, behind the safety of an acacia tree on the outskirts of the market, we stopped to catch our breath.

My heart was pounding. I was trembling from having committed my first crime.

Chanda's eyes popped open wide when she saw the stolen treasure in my shaking hands.

"Oh!" she said in a scared whisper. "Oh! Oh! Oh! What did you do?" She looked at me in shock.

"These are for you," I said, offering them to her with a shaky smile. "You can have your own red sandals too."

It took a whole hour to convince my friend to take those shoes, but finally, she did.

I never knew if Chanda dared to wear those new slippers of hers because that was the last I saw of her for a very long time.

And also because the very next day, the world as I'd known it ended.

Chapter EIGHT

T he day my world ended started innocently enough.

"Get in the car, Asha," my father said, hauling the family suitcase into the trunk.

I jumped inside our little Fiat, carrying my backpack filled with more books than clothes, and rolled down the window. Next to me was a stack of Tupperware, each holding twelve tiny cakes I could bite down in one minute or less.

"Don't eat these now," my mother said, startling me. She reached through my window and deposited a brown paper bag full of onion buns in the backseat, next to the cake containers. Normally, it took an iron will to not open the cake boxes, especially the one with the dark chocolate and creamy swirls on top. But that day, I had lost my appetite.

We were on our way to a safari, our annual week-long getaway hosted by the company where both my parents worked in Dar es Salaam.

I looked forward to it every year because it was rare my parents got away from their research and endless talk of mining, sanitation, and environmental devastation. I knew their work was important, but sometimes it felt like they lived in their lab coats.

Every year, I circled the safari date on the fridge calendar using the biggest sharpie I could find. I packed my bag two weeks ahead and spent the rest of the time telling anyone who'd listen to me about my trip. Those were the days filled with sweet anticipation. I'd drift off to sleep at night dreaming of rhinos, zebras, elephants, and giraffes congregating around a water hole.

It was always exciting to pile into our trusty green car, happy we were heading far away from school.

But this year was different.

The adrenaline rush from my first ever attempt at crime had cooled and in its place, an uneasy feeling had settled in my stomach. It felt like

I'd started something, something unpleasant, that would come to haunt me. It was not a feeling I could ignore.

I tried to push these emotions of foreboding to the back of my mind and enjoy the ride. I stuck my face out the window to feel the wind and take in the fresh open air.

Once we left the city behind, there was nothing much to see other than remote villages dotted along the road. After a while, the villages disappeared and the only vista for miles was fields of dry grass on both sides of the road. From inside the car, it was hard to see how tall this grass truly was, but I found out when I needed an emergency bathroom break and had to push through the elephant-high grass.

We were three hours into our drive. Up front, my parents were talking in hushed tones about something at work. I was trying not to fall asleep in the back after stuffing myself with two onion buns.

It was late in the afternoon and the sun was a gigantic globe of fire on the horizon. The sky was painted in hues of red, yellow, and tangerine as if a firestorm was raging in the heavens.

To my child's eye, everything was big in Africa—the sun, the people, the animals, the trees, and, yes, even the grass. I remembered how this grassy landscape went on for hours like we were sailing through an endless green ocean. Tiring of it, I'd decided to take a nap when I spotted the baobab tree silhouetted against the disappearing sun.

I used to call these "upside-down trees" because of how their ancient, leafless branches twisted into spindly roots on top. These trees were immense—even elephants found shelter under them. That day, a troupe of sandy-colored antelope was standing silently under the giant baobab, their curved horns making them look magnificent yet menacing. Seeing wildlife on road trips was a rare treat. Seeing them under a baobab was even rarer.

My father slowed down, so we could take in the view. It was a magical scene. The antelope stood completely still, watching us, listening, only their ears twitching. They seemed to be anticipating something.

Then, without warning, they scattered in panic, jumping several feet high.

I watched them with my mouth open.

What frightened them? Was it the grunt of a cheetah? A sharp burst from our old car?

I remembered, fleetingly, the massive black jeep suddenly appearing next to us.

My father yelled. My mother screamed.

I looked at it in shock.

Where did that come from?

I barely registered the grinding of the jeep's tires and the loud crash as it hit us.

Then, I heard a loud bang. And another.

With a violent jolt, our small car swung sideways.

I remember little after that because we ended up in the dark thicket of the elephant grass. The jeep was pushing us. All I heard was the *swoosh* of the grass against the windows.

I covered my face with my hands and screamed. And screamed.

When the car stopped moving, and I finally pried my eyes open, a fire was raging around us, like someone had lit the dry grass.

I swiveled around in a panic, calling out to my parents.

But they were eerily silent up front.

• • • •

TO BE CONTINUED...

• • • •

Read the First Chapters of the Next Red Heeled Rebels Book Here.

Chapter One

Two hands yanked me out of the crumpled car. My back scraped against the mangled door, but I felt no pain.

I looked around in a shocked daze. Everything was a blur of smoke and crackling fire. I heard shouting nearby. The man in the Tanzanian patrol uniform let go of my arm and doubled over coughing. It was a rough, gagging cough. His face was glowing, not from sweat but from the reflection of fire.

That was when I felt the heat. The grass around us, tall enough to hide a fully-grown African elephant, was ablaze. The fire was climbing the acacia tree we'd hit moments earlier, its leaves curling inward in pain.

I gazed in horror at our small Fiat, engulfed in flames. There was a familiar shadow inside. A darkened head collapsed forward. Another shadow leaned against the steering wheel, now a ring of fire.

"Oh my god!"

I struggled to my feet.

"Get back!" someone yelled.

"Mama! Papa!"

I had to get to them. Save them.

Before I could do anything, the officer grabbed me by the arm and pulled me through the hot grass, half carrying, half dragging me like a rag doll. I kicked at the dirt and struggled all the way, almost losing my precious red sandals.

"Lemme go!" I screamed. He dumped me on the asphalt and flopped down beside me, one hand tightly on my shoulder, the other wiping his face which was drenched in sweat.

The crackle of fire and the blaring of sirens were getting louder. I felt hands pull me onto a stretcher. People were shouting at each other and at me. Someone was forcing me to lie down, hands on my shoulders pinning me down.

"No! Let me go!"

I fought to get up.

"Hatari!" a sharp voice said behind me. "Danger!"

The man who'd pulled me out of the car came over and reached for my hands. "Huwezi kwenda nyuma," he said in a soft voice, shaking his head. I didn't understand and not because I didn't know the language.

"But we've got to go back! Do something!"

I lunged forward. Hands clamped me down. The officer sighed and shook his head.

"Pole, pole," he said.

I stared at him through the smoky haze. I knew enough Swahili to understand he'd just said "sorry."

I collapsed. My mind was heavy, foggy. *This isn't happening. This is a nightmare. I'll wake up soon.*

But the fire was all around us now. I couldn't see our car anymore.

Then, the world went black.

• • • •

CHAPTER TWO

"What did the police say?" a female voice whispered in the dark.

"Tight-lipped, they were," another whispered back. "I overheard one of them say it was a good thing a highway patrol was on the road, or it could have been worse."

Who's talking? I couldn't see a thing, but the voices kept going.

"How much worse could it have got?"

"I don't know but it sounded serious, from the way they were saying."

"I tell you what I think, Rosa. These foreigners just don't know how to drive here, but nobody wants to say that."

"Tell me about it." A big sigh. "Every time we go on those safari roads, I tell my husband somebody should put up signs or someone will get killed one of these days."

"If we had signs for lions, do you think tourists would stay away? They'd follow it with their fancy cameras, I tell you."

"Only the white muzungus will do that."

"Have you not seen those buses full of Chinese these days? Even the Wahindi are running around with their cameras, I tell you."

"Well, the good Lord was looking over this little Wahindi. She'll heal."

"Why don't we call that hindu priest to come and talk to her?"

"How do you know her church? Maybe she's buddhist, or christian or maybe even muslim. You never know these days."

"Well, we need someone to bless her parents."

Bless her parents? I pried my eyes open and was immediately blinded by a fluorescent light. I shut my eyes back tightly.

"The girl's up!"

"Call the doctor!"

I opened my eyes cautiously this time, to see two Tanzanian nurses in starched white aprons and stiff caps standing on either side of my bed. They were staring at me like I was an alien. I stared back. They couldn't have looked more different from each other. One was short and stout, and the other was thin and tall.

I looked around. We were in a small, windowless room. I was on a hospital bed with beeping machines surrounding me. On the wall in front was a wildlife calendar with a photo of a sandy-colored impala leaping over a bush, its long, black horns leading the charge. I did a double take. That reminded me of something, something urgent, but for the life of me, I couldn't think of what it was.

A shiver ran through me. This place was cold, sterile, and smelled of disinfectant like they'd scrubbed everything down with bleach. Something nipped at my arm. I looked down to see a gangly plastic tube sticking to my forearm. What's this? I pulled my arms up and instantly, a searing pain rushed through my body.

"Aaargh." I struggled to get up. "Where am I?" I spoke but heard only a strange, raspy sound. I put my hand on my throat. My back hurt and my legs felt heavy. Something somewhere was hurting badly, and tears welled up in my eyes.

"Now, now, take care, my dear," the stout nurse said, coming closer and putting a hand on my shoulder. Her hand felt warm to the touch.

"Don't pull on these," the other nurse said, fixing the IV bag. "These are for your own good. See, you're already feeling better, no?"

"Where's Mama?" I croaked. My throat was drier than the Sahara.

"Relax. No talking. You need rest," the plump nurse said, pushing a button on the side of the bed to bring it upright. In her hand was a plastic cup with a bent straw in it. "You'll be just fine," she said, pushing my long hair back. "This'll help. Drink."

I reached for the cup with shaking hands and put my lips on the straw. As they watched me silently, I took a tiny sip of the water.

The black phone by the door rang. The skinny nurse ran to pick it up and talked into it, nodding every few seconds, saying, "Yes, Doctor. Yes, Doctor." The plump nurse started to bustle around the room, taking readings from the screens and writing on charts.

I sat motionless with the cup in my hands, trying to make sense of what had happened, why I was here. Suddenly, a fiery image sprang to mind. It was of our green car in flames with the shadows of my parents inside. Unconscious.

My body went numb. Panicked thoughts came rushing in like a sandstorm in a desert, roaring, swirling, filling every crevice of my mind.

Mama! Papa! Did they get away? Are they okay? Oh, my god. Where are they?

My mind reeled. I remembered how I'd begged them to go on this safari, how I'd sniveled like a spoiled brat. I remembered the day before, how my best girlfriend, Chanda, and I had disappeared for hours in the

Uhuru market and worried them sick. It was also that morning I'd committed a crime, my first crime, a misdeed only Chanda knew about and one I'd regret for the rest of my life.

Mama always said karma never forgets.

The plump nurse turned and noticed my ashen face.

"Where's my mother?" I squeaked the words.

She set her chart on the side table and walked a slow deliberate walk toward my bed. Something in her face told me I didn't want her to answer my question. I didn't want her to speak. I pulled back. She leaned in and wrapped me in a hug. When she told me I wasn't going to see my parents again, I wanted to cry, scream, but I couldn't even breathe.

I made the accident happen. I'm the one who made them die.

I pulled away and threw up over the side of the bed. I didn't care I was spraying my sickly vomit on her pristine white skirt.

* * * *

CHAPTER THREE

"She's just a child," whispered the voice of the plump nurse, whom I knew as Nurse Elizabeth now. "Think of that before you make the decision."

I sat up in bed and looked around me. I'd just woken from a drug-induced sleep and was still drowsy. The voices were coming from the room next to mine, where the nurses kept their medical and bandage supplies and had a desk to write their charts and reports.

"This is not my decision, mesdames," a man replied.

I recognized that voice. It was Mr. Mudenda, the children's psychologist assigned to me. He was a small man with a pleasant face who'd visited me every afternoon for an hour, for the past two weeks. He was the only person, other than the cleaning lady, who came without a stethoscope around his neck. He shared stories about his family and told me about his eldest son, Peace, a year older than me, who went to a public school in town.

Sometimes, when Mr. Mudenda didn't have time to drop his son off at home, he'd bring him in, together with several books they'd picked out for me from the town library. As Mr. Mudenda inquired about my health, Peace would sit quietly on the bench outside the room, engrossed in his own book, his oversized spectacles threatening to fall off at any moment.

When I asked about the boy, Mr. Mudenda regaled with pride that Peace was at the top of his class, a chess prodigy, and even two grades ahead of his age group. I wished Peace would come in and chat but he never did. Other than an initial hello, he kept to himself. Instead, it was Mr. Mudenda's soothing voice and stories that put me to sleep every night.

Though I'd known Mr. Mudenda for only two weeks, he was all I had now. That first day, he came over with a book and sat next to my bed and read while I slipped in and out of consciousness, throwing up every few hours till I could vomit no more.

The nurses had their hands full with patients in far more serious conditions than I was. They didn't have time to pay attention to a child who felt worse in her heart than in her body, so it was Mr. Mudenda who stayed with me till dawn the next morning. After a few days, I came to trust him so much that I almost told him my terrible secret of crime.

"The police are still investigating, you know," Nurse Rosa, the thin nurse, was saying. "They'll want to talk to her."

My heart skipped a beat. They know what I did? I strained to listen.

"It's the police telling me to send the girl away," Mr. Mudenda said. "Besides, she can't stay here forever."

"But you can't ship off a little one just like that," Nurse Elizabeth said.

"It's for her own safety," Mr. Mudenda replied.

What does that mean?

"This is not the first time they had trouble," he continued. "Remember the dead Swedish scientist they found in the desert last year? He worked for Environ Africa as well, and he complained about the same problems in his letters to the newspapers. There will be an investigation, and it's going to be up to the commissioner now."

"Oh, my, my," Nurse Elizabeth said. "What's the world coming to these days?"

"The mining companies have long hands, and they don't like it when others meddle in their affairs," Mr. Mudenda said.

"They have all the money," Nurse Rosa said in a disapproving voice. "And we know where half of that ends up, don't we? Right in the pockets of our politicians."

I no longer followed the conversation. I shook my head from side to side to clear the heavy fog of drugs from my mind.

"What's her official status?" Nurse Elizabeth was asking. "Didn't she say her father's Indian and her mother's from Sri Lanka or somewhere like that?"

Their voices were getting lower. I leaned toward the door.

"According to the documents I received, she was born in Kenya," Mr. Mudenda said, rustling papers.

"A Kenyan citizen then?" Nurse Rosa asked.

"From what the police sent me, the parents were expatriate contractors." Mr. Mudenda spoke slowly as if he was reading something. "They moved around the region, but they had no residential papers from anywhere. The only things we have are copies of their passports kept at the company."

"What about a birth certificate?" Nurse Rosa asked.

"They've asked the Kenyan authorities, but that will take time. In the meantime, she doesn't belong anywhere, I'm afraid."

"Tsk. Poor girl. She must be ten, not even," Nurse Rosa said.

"Eleven, I think," Mr. Mudenda said. More rustling of papers.

Hey, I'm twelve now and that's almost thirteen.

I peeked over the bed. My ruby red sandals, the last birthday gift from my parents, were still there. They looked worn and dusty now, though I'd only got them a few days ago.

"What about school? Doesn't she go to the international school?" Nurse Rosa asked.

"That's a boarding school, isn't it?" Nurse Elizabeth said. "Maybe she can stay there for a while."

My heart dropped. I detested being at school during the day. I hated being the odd one out, the one everyone picked on. I couldn't imagine living there around the clock, especially without my parents to escape to. I shook my head silently. No, please no.

"Who's going to pay for that expensive school?" Mr. Mudenda asked. "The company promised only to take care of the funeral arrangements and her trip back."

Trip? Back?

"She tells us her home is here," Nurse Elizabeth said. "Let's see what a foster home could do, at least."

A wave of nausea washed over me. I pulled the blanket to my chin and curled my legs under me. Part of me didn't want to hear this any-more. Another part wanted to run into that room and demand to know what they were planning to do with me.

"Mesdames," my social worker said. "She does have a family, and as far as the authorities are concerned, that is where she has to go."

"Hmph!" Both nurses snorted at the same time.

"Didn't they say they didn't want the half-breed? That is what I heard," Nurse Rosa said with a huff.

"Yes, think of that now, Mr. Mudenda," Nurse Elizabeth said.

"Whether they like it or not, they'll have to take the girl," Mr. Mudenda said. "And Asha will have to adjust."

Adjust to what? My head was hurting.

"Habari!"

Someone else had entered the room. I heard the usual Swahili pleas-antries and a man's deep voice, a voice that was in charge.

"Did you tell the kid it's an accident?" the man barked.

I craned my neck to look, but couldn't see a thing.

"Don't worry, sir. I'm handling this the best way I can." Mr. Mudenda sounded strained now.

"Funeral arrangements will be made here by the company, two days from now," the man said.

"I'll take the girl with me," Mr. Mudenda said. "She will need company."

"Shouldn't we send the bodies back to the family?" Nurse Elizabeth asked.

"They do not want them," the man replied.

"Oh!" Nurse Elizabeth gasped.

"Tsk. Tsk. Tsk." Nurse Rosa always clicked her tongue when she wasn't happy.

I looked at the impala calendar on the wall where Nurse Rosa checked the days off every day. My parents would be buried on a Sunday.

A flood of memories came to me.

Sunday was our family day. It was the day my mother baked and I became her sous chef, piping creamy swirls onto little cakes. I'll never forget the heavenly baking smells that wafted through our home those quiet Sunday mornings when we'd brew cups of steaming Ceylon tea and sit at the kitchen table with my father to taste my mother's latest creations.

No matter how bad the week had been, Sundays made the world all right again.

"What kind of family is this, you have found?" Nurse Elizabeth's angry voice came from the room.

"Don't be so quick to judge," Mr. Mudenda said. "They've been in Africa for the past twelve years. Probably no one even knew this girl was alive."

"We can't fly the bodies anyway," the strange man said. He didn't seem to be making any effort to lower his voice. "I was at the mortuary when they brought them in. Oh, man. Not something you want to see, I can tell you that."

"At least the commissioner said he will look into this business," Mr. Mudenda said. "I just hope the company doesn't start lobbying like they always do."

"Those bastards," the man said. "Always interfering with our investigations."

Silence.

"Are you going to escort us to the airport after the funeral?" Mr. Mudenda asked.

"We're going to drive you there, my friend," the man replied with a chuckle. "Only the president gets an escort."

. . . . .

CONTINUE THE ADVENTURE...

Would you like to know what happens to Asha next?

She'd just survived a fiery car crash in the middle of nowhere. Both her parents are gone but that's nothing compared to what she was going to face next...

The Girl Who Ran Away is a gritty tale of crime and betrayal that will take you on a roller-coaster ride from the streets of Tanzania to a seaside village in India, to a ritzy North American city where Asha thinks she's finally safe, but learns too late she can trust no one.

Get the multiple award-winning next book in the series, The Girl Who Ran Away here: www.RedHeeledRebels.com[1]

---

1.   http://www.redheeledrebels.com/

. . . .

THANK YOU READING THIS story!

Did you enjoy the story?

Your thoughts mean a lot to me and honest reviews are invaluable. They help me enter this book in international promotions and reach a global audience.

If you'd like to support an indie author who's propelling her own way, you can leave an honest review here:

Review this Book on Your Favorite Book Platform.[2]
https://books2read.com/The-Girl-Who-Crossed-the-Line

Thank you so much.

---

2.   https://books2read.com/The-Girl-Who-Crossed-the-Line

The Red Heeled Rebels Thriller Series

I n a world where justice no longer prevails, six iron-willed women rally together to seek vengeance on those who stole their humanity.

This is a story where the thrill of *Kill Bill* meets the wrath of *The Girl with the Dragon Tattoo.*

If you like gripping thrillers with flawed but gutsy heroines, vigilante action in exotic locales and twists that leave you at the edge of your seat, you'll love these books by multiple award-winning Canadian novelist, Tikiri Herath.

Pick up the Red Heeled Rebels books for a heart-pounding international adventure without having to get a passport or even buy an airline ticket!

• • • •

WHAT READERS ARE SAYING on Amazon and Goodreads:

- "Fast-paced and exciting!"

- "An exciting and thought-provoking book."

- "A wonderful story! I didn't want to leave the characters."

- "I couldn't put down this exciting road trip adventure with a powerful message."

- "Another award-worthy adventure novel that keeps you on the edge of your seat."

- "A heart-stopping adventure. I just couldn't put the book down till I finished reading it."

• "Kept me mesmerized and captivated with the rich descriptions which made me feel like I was actually inside the story."

• "This is a fantastic read that will have you traveling the globe. I absolutely loved this book. You won't be able to put it down!"

• "A real page turner and international thriller. Reminds me of why I've always loved to read. Because I can visit worlds and places I wouldn't ordinarily get to see."

To learn more about this addictive series, go to www.RedHeeledRebels.com[1]

. . . .

PREQUEL: THE GIRL WHO Crossed the Line

A reckless girl. A grave mistake. A fateful destiny.

All she wanted was to belong. Then, she committed an unforgivable crime...

. . . .

BOOK ONE: THE GIRL Who Ran Away

An estranged orphan. A treacherous plot. A perilous journey that could kill her.

She'd just survived a fiery car crash in the middle of nowhere. Both her parents are dead, but that's nothing compared to what she would face next...

. . . .

BOOK TWO: THE GIRL Who Made Them Pay

---

1.   http://www.RedHeeledRebels.com

A kidnapped friend. A forbidden house. A precarious journey to escape their captors.

They are fleeing a fate worse than death. They think they're finally safe in London, when one of them is snatched into a waiting black cab. And now, she will do anything to find her friend...

• • • •

BOOK THREE: THE GIRL Who Fought to Kill

A lost cousin. A heinous crime. An impossible rescue that risks it all.

She was ready to cross oceans to hunt down her stolen cousin. But she didn't know the terrifying stakes waiting for her on the other side that will test her resolve and courage...

• • • •

BOOK FOUR: THE GIRL Who Broke Free

A sweet sixteenth birthday banquet. A missing diplomat's daughter. A menacing family secret.

She thought she'd finally made it when she was invited to cater for the swankiest party in upscale Manhattan. But she didn't realize the birthday girl's family has other plans and the banquet is a ruse for something more perilous than she could ever imagine...

• • • •

BOOK FIVE: THE GIRL Who Knew Their Names

A glittering Hollywood gala. An actress with a dark vendetta. A cold-blooded murder among the stars.

She thought she'd snagged the most coveted catering job in Los Angeles, and a chance to meet A-list celebrities. But she didn't realize she was about to confront the most powerful predator in town on her first day...

• • • •

BOOK SIX: THE GIRL Who Never Forgot

A girl from the swamps. A family gripped by darkness. A killer on the loose at the Mardi gras.

She was invited to cater a lavish ball where New Orleans' blue-blooded families celebrated Mardi gras in style, away from the cacophony of common street parades. But she didn't realize a murderer was lurking in the shadows, waiting to frame her for their deed...

• • • •

AWARDS & PRAISE FOR The Red Heeled Rebels books:

- Grand Prize Award Finalist - 2019 Eric Hoffer Award, USA
- First Horizon Award Finalist - 2019 Eric Hoffer Award, USA
- Honorable Mention General Fiction - 2019 Eric Hoffer Award, USA
- Winner First-In-Category - 2019 Chanticleer Somerset Award, USA
- Semi-Finalist - 2020 Chanticleer Somerset Award, USA
- Winner in 2019 Readers' Favorite Book Awards, USA
- Winner of 2019 Silver Medal - Excellence E-Lit Award, USA
- Winner in Suspense Category - 2018 New York Big Book Award, USA
- Finalist in Suspense Category - 2018 & 2019 Silver Falchion Awards, USA
- Honorable Mention - 2018-19 Reader Views Literary Classics Award, USA
- Publisher's Weekly Booklife Prize – 2018 - USA

About the Author

Tikiri Herath is a multiple-award-winning Canadian author.
Born in Sri Lanka, a tropical island in the Indian Ocean, she spent her childhood in South East Africa, and has lived and worked in Southeast Asia, Continental Europe, and North America.
She started her adult life as a lone immigrant girl, but went on to receive a bachelor's degree from the University of Victoria, British Columbia and a master's degree from the Solvay Business School in Brussels.
For fifteen years, she worked in risk management in the intelligence and defense sectors, including in the Canadian Federal Government and at NATO.
Tikiri's an adrenaline junkie who has rock climbed, bungee jumped, rode on the back of a motorcycle across Quebec, flown in an acrobatic airplane upside down, and parachuted solo.
When she's not writing or plotting another thriller scene, you'll most probably find her baking in her kitchen with a glass of red wine in hand and jazz playing in the background.
To say hello and get free travel stories from around the world, go to www.TikiriHerath.com.[1]

---

1. http://www.TikiriHerath.com